AF484183
BIG BREASTED VAMPIRE SLUTS 
NEO GRINDHOUSE
Drive In finger bang!
Touch 'em
Taste 'em
Ain't no badder BITCH!
BRIDGET CHASE

BIG BREASTED VAMPIRE SLUTS

Bridget Chase

Chapter 1

Dust swirled in the purple plum sunset. A distant light beckoned.

The 'pimped out' retro-fitted NASA rover, sped through the small village.

With the sun below the horizon, their destination, nicknamed Turquoise Palace, sparkled in the dying light.

(♪ Synthwave 80's music played ♪)

Running lights danced on Cosmic Ray's visor as he drove.

The rover was refabricated, resembling a sleek race car. The tires chewed the gravel.

He strangled the wheel. A tight harness held him to his seat. The vehicle bounced.

"Fifteen minutes till arrival," Cosmic Ray said over the intercom.

The team member beside him, Scarlet, nodded. Her eyes were fixed on the glowing alien structure.

Ray looked in the rearview mirror. His other teammate sat unmoving.

In the back, Agent Repeat thought about the mission. Repeat was sure this was a suicide run. He looked out the side window. Endless woods containing hell waited. Repeat wondered what the two others had done to deserve being sent to Transylvania?

∞

"Play it again."

Maloy watched. He hardly breathed.

Diggs tapped the screen.

It was footage from the team's helmet cam.

"OH GOD! FUCK!" the guy screamed.

Their flashlights swirled over endless dark crevices.

Red eyes burned in the darkness.

Blurry things were there and then gone.

"This is Cosmic Ray's helmet cam?" Maloy asked.

"Yes sir," Diggs replied.

Ray spun.

Quick movements darted in front of him.

A woman screamed.

Ray opened fire.

Dusts and debris swirled across the camera lens.

Something moved in the mist.

"FUCK!" Ray shouted. Static abused the audio. His rifle flashed.

Something danced around in the dark fog.

"Pause it!" Maloy said.

The video stopped.

Diggs and Maloy leaned forward.

The screen reflected on his glasses

"I'll be damned," Diggs said.

"Fuck me." Maloy rubbed his slack jaw, "What are we going to tell the Defense Board?".

The image was blurred, but there was no denying what they saw.

"Big breasted Vampire Sluts," Maloy said.

∞

(♪ Badass 'trance inducing' Synthwave music played ♪)

The red two door 1988 Pontiac Fiera raced through the empty night.

The dark forest- an empty expanse closed in.

With the windows down, the cool air blew over Stud's tense face.

Music blared, rising into the abyss of the night.

Notes and rhythm, wrung images from Stud's mind.

Greif pulled him. Questions drew him.

The headlights cut twin dragons out of the void.

All alone on the road, the world didn't exist. Reality became the ten feet of concrete illuminated by the headlights, and the pain gripping his heart.

CHAPTER 2

SLIK SLAK! Cosmic Ray hit the dark wolf in the face. It stumbled back. He leveled his rifle and fired.

CLAK, CLAK, CLAK! Bullets blew holes in its chest.

The beast roared.

Scarlet came to Ray's side after shooting down a blood thirsty bat. "We're fucked," she shouted.

The wolf, that walked on two legs, fell.

Ray moved quickly to its side. He squeezed the trigger unloading the whole mag into the things face.

Blood popped and flesh tore. Part of its nose ripped off and white skull crunched with holes.

The beast snarled.

CLAK, CLAK, CLAK! Scarlet shot at the swarming bats.

"Thing won't fucking die," Ray said.

The beast climbed to its feet as Ray reloaded.

Lighting bolted through the night sky. Water raged at the perilous rocks beside them.

The wolf ran forward.

Ray raised his rifle. When the wolf grabbed hold, he rolled back. Placing a foot to the wolf's stomach, he threw it over the side of the cliff.

Off in the distance torches burned along the walls of a small village.

"Let's move," Scarlet said. One of her bullets tore through the eye of a bat. Black yogurt exploded from its head.

The two of them hurried along the wooded path. Small steams and rocky hills slowed their progress.

∞

The office was silent.

General Brick got up from his chair. He walked to the window. Pulling down the blinds he peered out.

Darkness weighed heavy on the landscape.

His eyes scanned the dark woods.

Only an hour ago, Maloy had shown him the footage. It was the militaries worst nightmare.

General Brick knew about NASA's discover of 'big breasted vampire sluts' on the dark side of the moon.

But, now they were here, and in Transylvania of all places. He came back to his desk and sat.

Opening a bottom drawer, he pulled out a bottle of whiskey and a single glass.

Maybe I... He didn't' know what to do.

His team was gone and he was here, in this small military outpost, only miles way.

General Brick kicked back the whiskey. It burned his throat. A fogginess came over his mind.

He jumped when a hand caressed his shoulder.

The General quickly turned. He came face to face with gorgeous big tits.

He looked up. "Who, who?"

The gorgeous woman leaned down. Her cleavage was cupped in a dark leather corset. They were pressed together and in his face.

Her body was one of 'nut busting' dreams. Slim waist, provocative hips, lips of an orgasm, and tits that make men rocket cum like the floods of Noah.

"You reek of fear and…"

She leaned closer.

He felt her eyelashes tickle his cheek.

"Arousal."

The General lost his breath when her hand cupped his crotch.

General Brick was old as fuck. Shit, his cock hadn't been touched by a woman in, fuck all, twenty years.

"You're, you're, a vampire," he said.

She had dark sleek eyes that spoke of dick sucking and swallowing cum.

(♪ Heavy techno music faded in ♪)

Her hands moved to his belt. She licked her lips. Two white fangs peeked out. She moaned.

The general sat frozen. He was scared but FUCK! Something kept him from moving.

His cock was electric. His zipper went down.

She tossed her beautiful dark hair to one side.

The general starred down at her cleavage.

The skin was delicate, pale, soft, and fuck, probably the most perfect set of tits ever created.

Her fingers wrapped his dick and she pulled it from his boxers.

The General's breath went shaky.

Uhh," he moaned as she stroked.

She squeezed her tits together and used both hands to massage.

The general was in ecstasy. He reached forward. His hand touched the soft skin of her tits. Instinctively the general slipped his hand into the forbidden cup.

The woman leaned down.

A warm ring encircled his cock. Her wet tongue flicked- begging his head.

"Ahh... ahhh," The general's balls rose. Cum raged, about to explode.

Then...

∞

Maloy sat at his desk.

A sudden terrible scream drew his attention.

It sounded like the general.

He got up from his desk. Opening his office door- the hall was dark. At the end, a light shone under the general's door.

Hmm. He walked forward slowly.

Reaching the door, he placed his ear to it.
Nothing.
Maloy knocked. "General Brick?" He waited.
(Knock, knock) "General?"
He opened the door.
Someone spoke.
The door closed behind him.

∞

The red Pontiac drifted and came to a stop in front of the small military outpost.
Gravel dust rose into the night.
Stud opened his door. His reeboks met the earth.
Stud was 'meant' to be played by the 'action super star' Sylvester Stallone. Unfortunately for the casting department, he was otherwise engaged.
Luckily, a strange series of events brought an unlikely actor to accept the leading role in this movie.
Hillary Clinton took the role of Stud. After losing the election, she pounded steroids, protein, and hit the gym. She wanted to finish out her life as the truest version of herself. Ms. Clinton had always envied Rambo. Secretly she wanted to be a ripped Alpha male.
Well, now she was, and she was ready to conquer Hollywood.
Stud looked around. It was fucking quiet. Maybe too fucking quiet.
He wore no shirt. His ripped pecs and hard abs were on display.

Hillary had worked hard to get pecks like that. Liposuction, hours in the gym, and still, she had to keep them permanently flexed, or else her 'pre sex change' woman 'flapjack' tits would show.

After his wife hadn't come home is two days, Stud came to the military outpost to get answers.

He and his wife, Scarlet, had been temporarily relocated to Transylvania when her NASA employer granted her a research position.

Stud went to the trunk of his car.

The light shone on an assortment of firearms and knives.

He grabbed a knife and assault rifle.

SLAM! The trunk closed and Stud walked up the steps to the door.

The foyer was deserted.

He checked his mag. CLICK!

Passing the front desk there were halls to both sides.

The lights were out.

Stud walked quietly.

He checked the whole east wing and nothing.

Going down the west hall, there was a door at the end. A strip of light shone below.

Stud readied his rifle.

He clutched the knob

(Turn)

A military man sat behind a desk. He was pale and slumped over.

A man in a white lab coat lay near the door. He seemed to be barely alive.

A woman, wearing gothic black shit, was kneeled over him and looked to be sucking his dick.

She slowly turned and looked to the door.

Blood coated her sexy lips.

The man's dick was shredded and dripped dark blood from deep punctures. His ball sack was ripped open and nuts had bloody holes in them.

"My god," Stud said.

The woman got to her feet and hissed.

It was then, that Stud realized what he saw. *A Vampire*!

CLAK, CLAK! He fired.

She dodged in supernaturally fast movements.

Stud was pushed back against the wall. Her hand clamped his throat.

He froze. She leaned close.

"What's this?" She sniffed. "Uhg," an unpleasant look came over her gorgeous face. "You're not a man," she said.

"Why, yes I am," Stud said offended.

"No, no, gross," the big breasted vampire backed up and let go.

Stud rubbed his neck. He flexed his pecs and raised his gun.

The vampire could see it. No erection was in his pants. Her tits could sense cocks anywhere. No, this was no man.

Stud fired CLAKKK KKKK KKK!

CRASH! The vampire lept out the window.

Stud lowered his gun. "Not a man? What a bitch."

A low mumble drew his attention.

Stud went to the side of the man on the ground.

"What happened here? What happened to my wife?" Stud asked.

The man had little life left. "Big breasted vampire sluts," the man said and died.

A messy pool of dark blood covered his crotch.

"My wife, Scarlet, what about my wife?" Stud shook the man's lifeless body.

Damn.

CHAPTER 3

He kicked open the door to a small store.

Cosmic Ray and Scarlet entered.

They made it out of the forest and now where making their way through a gothic medieval town.

"Care to purchase an item today?" A man wearing a grey robe approached and asked.

Ray looked at him in disbelief.

They were covered in dark matter, blood, sweat, and mud.

"Buy something," Ray said, "Fuck, how about a fucking phone?"

"So sorry, no phone here, sir," the man said.

Scarlet looked around. There wasn't shit inside that place except for a wood table. "Can we hide out in here for a while?" she asked.

"Certainly," the robed figure said.

Ray went to the table and set his gun down. "What the fuck is happening here?" he asked.

Scarlet removed her jumpsuit. Underneath she wore a tight white tank top and dark booty shorts.

Scarlet, played by Eva Mendez, let her hair down.

Ray couldn't help but gawk watching the rise of her 'Oh so delicious' tits and fall of her beautiful dark hair.

"Shit," she said, "I don't know. Everything was normal and then the sun went down."

"Ah," the robed man interrupted, "You should have known better than to travel during the cursed time."

"Cursed time?" Ray asked.

The old man said some shit. I won't bore you with the 'how and why'. Fuck, basically like Castlevania, shit was bad after dark.

The man told them the path to getting out of town.

Scarlet purchased a chain whip and some armor.

Ray stuck with his assault rifle.

Scarlet (Eva Mendes) put on her new breast plate. The hard plate cupped her tits and pressed them together. She then put on the pleated, studded, leather skirt. Slipping the arm guards on next, she then grabbed the whip and SNAP! Popped that fucker.

Ray's mouth hung open.

Fuck all, she was insanely beautiful.

Which, is pretty much why the casting director hired her. Ball busting bombshells sell lots of movie tickets.

Ray, played by Jason Stathem, pulled out a cigarette. He lit that bitch and watched the smoke drift. He was a fucking NASA astronaut. How he got assigned to this shit was a 'not so interesting' story. He wore a space suit on this mission. Why? Because NASA is a bureaucratic fucktard and only sends people on missions in the spacesuit.

It was currently dripping with gore.

SCRATCH, SCRATCH!

They looked to the old school wooden door.

"Oh, no," the store owner said, "You must go. You've brought them."

"We aren't going out there," Ray said, "Are you crazy?"

SMASH!

The stained-glass window in the back of the store shattered.

Half-naked women with flowing hair, black gypsy dresses, and razor claws came flying in.

Scarlet spun her whip.

∞

(♪ High energy Future wave music played ♪)

The woods were fucking hell.

Stud laid waste to the creatures that lurked there.

CLAKKK KKKK!

Fucking twelve werewolves charged.

He had shot each of them but his bullets seemed to do nothing but slow them down.

They dripped with blood and fury.

Snarls and snapping teeth abused the night.

CLAKKK KKKK!

Stud fired at one coming from behind.

The bullets ripped through its eye. The werewolf fell to a knee, shook its head, and then resumed the attack.

"Okay, time for plan B," Stud said.

He had no idea fucking werewolves would be between him and his wife, but shit, Stud was known as 'Stud' for a reason.

He reached in his pockets and pulled out sliver 'brass knuckles'. "You want to fuck with me, then come get it."

Lightning crawled across the purple canopy of the night sky.

The bloody beasts closed in.

WHACK SLIK SLAK!

Stud caught the first one in its face.

A second snapped at his neck.

Stepping back POW! Drove his fist into its stomach.

The (silver) brass knuckles destroyed the first werewolf's face. Half its skull crushed and then, in gooey blobs, dripped off.

His fist went through the second one's stomach.

A third came from behind. Stud back kicked.

It stumbled.

Leaping over its dying friend another werewolf flew at him.

Stud ducked. It SMACK! Hit the 'one' he had just kicked.

Now crouched, Stud struck upward. CLAK! His fist found a werewolf's jaw. BOOOM!

Bloody dark matter and jawbone popped like a firecracker in the strobing light of the sky.

It rained red blood.

He stood. Gore coated his face and chest.

Lightning flashed. Running toward him were four more were wolfs.

Stud took a defensive stance.

CHAPTER 4

The walls glowed.

Rein lay in her coffin.

Her eyes were closed. She wore a red robe. It was untied and she was completely naked underneath the silky fabric. The front was open exposing a soft bare breast.

After draining the 'aroused' blood from the two men at the government station and fleeing that strange he/she man with a gun, Rein had come back to her chamber to slumber.

Rein was played by the all too 'amazingly gorgeous' Noureen Dewulf. Yes, now you know what 'perfect tits' I had been describing earlier.

In her mind's eye, blood flowed and flooded the earth. Cocks lined the streets. As she walked, they all grew erect. When she stepped on them, they rocketed stringy cum. A smile curled her gorgeous lips. *Endless organs to drink from.*

∞

Hundreds of 'big breasted vampire sluts' sprinted down the cobbled street.

CLAKKK KKKKK!

Ray fired

SLAM! SLAK! Bullets ripped through their sexy bodies.

The slutty vampires wore 'marvelously revealing' gothic dresses. Some, tight leather corsets, others loose airy fabric so thin their erect nipples were visible.

Ray sprinted, slid across the ground, and fired.

Scarlet jumped over him, flipped, and landed. She snapped her whip. The leather cord wrapped a sultry vampire's neck.

SLAK! The whip ripped its head off.

The head soared and blood squirted.

SLAK, SLAK, SNAP! Scarlet cracked the whip. POW!

A laceration cut the cleavage of an impossible sexy vampire wearing a tight black dress.

The vampire hissed and recoiled. Her ass cheeks peeked out below the ultra-low hem of her dress. The vampire's huge tits spilled out over the low neckline.

Ray rolled.

He was swarmed. Four slutty women landed on top of him.

"Help!" he called out.

Scarlet turned. Her tits were amazing cupped in the 'sci fi medieval' chest plate. They were popping out. Eve Mendes played the role beautifully.

Gore speckled her cheeks. Her sexy lips were held fierce and her lithe body moved in alluring ultra-violent poses.

CRACK SNAP! Her whip pulled one off Ray. With a yank the vampire's arm tore off.

"Bitch," the slut said.

SLIK SLAK! Scarlet's whip popped two vampires in the face. Lacerations opened on their cheeks. They slinked away.

CLAKKKK KKKK KKKK! Ray unloaded his mag into one's stomach.

The vampire's tits bounced and slipped out of the corset's cups. They wiggled as she convulsed. The slut straddled Ray's lap. Dark matter rained down on him. She thrashed and grinded against his groin.

Ray grew erect.

She put her hands on his shoulders.

CLAKKKKKKKKK! He continued to fire, holding the rifle to her stomach.

She thrashed and bucked, moaning, and then …

The slutty vampire came hard. Her groin begging his manhood to erupt.

SNAP! Scarlet took the 'cumming' vampire's head off with the whip.

She helped Ray up.

"Thanks," he said. 'Blue balls' ached in his pants.

The slutty demons hissed. They moved in a circular around Ray and Scarlet.

The two of them got back to back.

Ray looked at the women's dark eyes and their long 'beyond black' eye lashes. Their lips were thick, soft cock massagers. The vampires all had amazing tits that made Ray's nuts want to pop like the big bang.

The slutty vampires' eyes all looked at him.

"Come too us Ray," they began to say seductively. Their body movements weren't aggressive anymore. Now they gyrated and pulling at their clothes.

"Don't listen," Scarlet said.

Ray was drawn in.

The vampires began to release their tits. Hundreds of gorgeous cupcake breasts and caramel nipples begged him.

Ray took a step.

"Ray, no," Scarlet said. She grabbed his shoulders and held him.

"I…" His eyes couldn't leave the vampires bodies. *Holy shit*!

The vampires pulled up their dresses and rubbed between their legs. Some teased- pulling their panties low showing off hairless pussies.

Ray's cock was a magnet. Shit, every blood cell was no longer blood, but cum, that begged for release.

He pushed against Scarlet.

"Come to us," they said. The sluts began sucking their fingers like a cock. Their eyes said they would suck him to completion until his cock was soft and drained.

He couldn't help it.

"Ray, no," Scarlet held his arm.

He walked forward and pulled away.

"Yes come, cum."

Ray walked to them and then POUNCE! They piled on him.

First, Ray screamed, but then he moaned.

Vampires went for his neck, thighs, and many devoured his genitals.

Blood leaked out across the ground.

Scarlet stood unmoving. She didn't know how she would get out of this.

∞

The moon was powerful but Rein was even stronger.

Her coffin lid was open and her legs hung over the side. She rubbed her clit and toyed with her nipples.

In the glowing cathedral were hundreds of open coffins.

All the slutty vampires played with themselves.

Together they built their energy and drew all the sleeping men, in town, to them.

A man at home in bed saw bouncing tits and hugging wet flesh. He got out from bed in a daze and walked into the night.

The man joined the group of men, all walking together down the street. Half asleep their erect dicks led them forward.

(♪ Dark 'Gaming Mix' Synthwave music faded in ♪)

Rein was growing to a climax. Slippery fluid coated her fingers. She could see the marching army of delicious agitated cocks coming. Rein licked her lips. Tonight, she and her species would feast.

∞

Scarlet let her breath out. She watched as the vampires left.

Where are they going? She decided it didn't matter. Now was her time to escape.

She looked away from Ray's body. It was gore- worse than any horror movie.

She ran down the dark gothic street of Transylvania.

Torches on the buildings suddenly lit. They ignited- racing past her.

Strange. She moved forward.

Then she saw, *shit no*.

Hundreds of men. Most undressed and some still undressing; headed towards her.

Scarlet didn't know if she would be safe passing through.

"Scarlet!" a voice called.

She turned.

"Stud? Oh my god! Stud!" She ran towards her husband.

"Shhh, shh," he came around the corner.

Scarlet jumped into his arms. Her 'all I've ever wanted' tits pressed against his ripped chest.

Hillary felt a stir in her fabricated balls.

"How did you?" Scarlet was shocked.

"There is no time," he said. "We need to get out of here."

They slipped into the alley.

"Did you see all those men coming?" she asked.

"Yeah."

"We need to stop them. They will all be killed."

Stud thought for a moment. He didn't know how many vampires were inside. "Fine, he said. "Follow me."

They ran to the next building and went in.

Chapter 5

SMASH, CRASH! Stud used his rifle butt and broke everything in the room.

"What are you doing?" Scarlet asked.

He ran around and collected the hearts and coin icons that appeared.

"If we are taking down this horde of Vampires, then we need to upgrade." SMASH! Stud broke a vase.

"Okay," Scarlet said. She broke a candle holder with her whip.

BING! A heart appeared. Scarlet walked through it.

"Let's go," Stud said. "We have many places to trash tonight."

∞

The door was held open by Trite. She was one of Rein's subordinates.

The men walked in. Naked, with their eyes glazed over, they entered the sanctuary.

Immediately the men paired up with big breasted women. Kissing and groping ensued.

They fell to the floor in the throes of passion.

Moans and sucking sound were the 'Sunday Choir' in this large room.

A thick hairy man came up to Rein. His cock was ridged and twitching.

She embraced him and took him to the ground.

Rein slid her tongue down his chest as he trembled in delight.

She moved down to his manhood.

The man spasmed.

Rein sucked at the hot juices.

∞

(♪ Rammstein 'Du Hast' faded in ♪)

CLICK CLAK! Stud slid the magazine in.

Scarlet coiled her new diamond whip. She had also purchased a cross bow which was now on her back.

Stud turned. He wore black tactical gear. A red bandana was tied around his forehead. "Ready?"

"Let's do it," Scarlet said.

BOOOOOM!

The castle door exploded into 'fucked up' splintered pieces.

(Hiss!) The vampires turned from their prey.

Moonlight streamed in through the stained-glass window. They depicted some sort of Vampire nirvana.

Red light played across the ground.

Stud opened fire. CLAKKKKK!

Scarlet ran past him. CRACK! She popped her whip.

The vampires screamed in rage.

Many half naked vampire sluts jumped and hung from the ceiling.

The walls shimmered in alien iridescence.

Some of the sexy vampire bitches flexed. Their arms glowed electric blue. ZAP! Fire balls came out.

Stud slid between a set. Coming to a knee he fired.

SLIK, SLAK! Two vampires' heads snapped back. Blood rocketed from their faces. Their sexy tits bounced as they fell.

SNAP, CRACK! Scarlet whipped back and forth. Vampires screamed. Lacerations opened on their bodies.

A group of twenty swarmed Stud.

He held them all off, kicking, and punching.

One climbed his back. Stud put his rifle under her chins and pulled the trigger.

Her head popped like a virgin's first penetration.

He came back with an elbow to another.

The vampire's gorgeous golden hair whipped.

More fireballs came and stud rolled.

Scarlet soared in the air. SNAP! Her whip wrapped vampires' necks and tore them off.

Rein stood at the top of the stairs. She watched her species being murdered. *They will pay*.

She took off her robe.

CLAKKKKK! Stud spun in a circle.

Vampires fell all around him.

They suddenly stopped attacking and began squeezing their tits.

Stud watched, *what are they doing*?

The vampires gyrated.

Scarlet had seen this before. She took a wide stance and summoned the electric lighting from the earth through her feet.

The current sizzled over her body.

Scarlet became like lighting and just as fast. She flew through the huge group of masturbating vampires.

Her whip glowed and moved supernaturally fast. Scarlet shot around the room like a lion in a field of mice.

Screams and blood flew. Body parts fell to the ground.

Rein summoned her dark Lord. A phantasm appeared behind her. A huge demon with long curling horns. It glowed red.

"Enter my lord and stop this," Reni said. She was completely nude.

The camera man filming hoped no one on set saw the heavy erection in his pants. The camera panned up Rein's rib cage and caught a 'nut busting' shot of her perfect springy tits. No, no man had ever seen such a perfect set of breasts.

With a whoosh the demon entered Rein's body. She jumped and glided down to the sanctuary floor.

A hail of gunfire moved through the room and Scarlet took down the last few remaining vampires.

The director of the movie shed a tear. It was too sad seeing all those perfectly gorgeous sluts dead. He had hopes for creating a sequel, but we will get to that soon.

Scarlet breathed heavily. She was covered in blood and sweat. She heard something land behind her and turned.

Stud shouldered his gun.

"You mother fuckers," Rein said. "Well no matter. There are plenty more of us on the dark side of the moon. We will come back and destroy you all." She raised her hand and a set of four fireballs came from her finger tips.

Scarlet jumped and Stud rolled.

CLAKKKK KKKKK He opened fire.

The bullets bounced of some forcefield around Rein.

Rein's hair rose above her head as she floated. Her tits floated like zero gravity.

Scarlet let loose her whip.

SNAP CRACK!

The forcefield sizzled and Rein laughed.

"Now what?" Scarlet asked Stud.

He checked his mags. *I'm almost out.*

Then he came up with a plan. "Get your cross bow ready. We only get one chance," Stud said.

"What are you going to do?" Scarlet asked.

"Just be ready."

Scarlet dropped her whip and readied the cross bow with a 'wooden stake' arrow.

Rein smiled down at them.

Stud approached.

"I know we interrupted your feast. I have an offering for you. I know how you like cocks, and I got the best one around." Stud unzipped his pants.

Now, we know Hillary Clinton played this role. Her sex change went reasonably well but by no means well enough to show on screen. So, just like in 'Boogie Nights' with Mark Walhberg, they covered her small dick with a large dildo.

His pants and boxers hugged his ankles. Stud's cock hung to his knees.

Oh my god! Rein's eyes went huge. She had never seen such a beauty. This was the most glorious cock ever. She licked her lips. Desire burned in her demon chest, behind huge perfect tits, that men dreamed of covering with stringy white frosting.

Rein floated to the ground.

Stud moved his legs wide. "Come and get it."

Rein walked forward.

"Stop," Stud said. "Crawl on your knees."

Rein was hypnotized. She got down on all fours. Her tits swayed, hanging from her chest, as her arms moved.

Rein approached. She rubbed her cheek and face on his cock like a kitten in need of attention.

Stud became aroused by her display of overwhelming desire. He knew he had her.

Stud's head rose in front of her eyes.

Rein opened her mouth revealing fangs.

"Now," Stud said.

Scarlet, down on one knee, fired.

The wooden arrow flew across the room.

SLAK!

"AHHHH!" Rein cried out and fell backwards. She clawed at the cock as she fell away. *I want it, I want it.*

"Umph" she laid on the ground.

Stud walked forward.

Rein looked up to the beautiful penis hanging there and then to the gun aimed at her.

CLAK!

CHAPTER 6

Neon lights from the street streamed in through the blinds.

Stud and Scarlet moved under the covers on the bed.

He sucked her strawberry nipple while burying himself deep inside her.

Scarlet moaned.

After killing Rein and the vampires, they had come home to their hotel room.

Scarlet and Stud had taken a shower. The blood and grim rolled off their bodies and down the drain.

Stud had watched the movement of Scarlet's sensual body. Which led to a long fucking session.

∞

He kicked back his beer.

Bill looked at his wasted face in the bar mirror. *Shee-it I'm old as fuck.*

He had come in every night since Hillary had left. To make things worse, she was now a man.

Well, fuck her, I don't need her.

A warm feminine hand slid over his. "Can I buy you another?" A female voice asked.

Bill looked up.

It was a beautiful woman with tits like the sun.

"Sure," he said.

After a few more beers, they wound up in the backseat of Bill's limo.

His eager cock slipped inside of her.

The gorgeous woman's pussy was warm and tight. Then...

"ARGH" Bill screamed.

Razor sharp things closed on his cock.

"YES!" she said and moaned. The woman pulled up all her hair with both hands and bounced on his lap.

Her pussy drank of Bill's aroused blood.

The woman leaned down. She put her hand to his shoulders and smiled.

Razor fangs showed behind her lips.

His cock was drained, Bill's last word were, "Fuck, big breasted vampire sluts are here."

The sexy vampire attacked.

The limo rocked and Bill's hand struck the window.

A bloody smear was left. His hand disappeared.

Well, that's that. Vampires, tits, and slutty action. Who the fuck needs Harry Potter and his impotent wand? Hmm, should a sequel be in the works? Maybe. Visit my website for coming soon titles, new releases, and other author shit. Thanks for reading. Leave and awesome review about the importance of delicious tits in literature. On to my next book and a buffet of sexy women.

https://chasebridget.wordpress.com